MW00904578

this book belongs to:

_____

ALOHASAURUS

written by **Vera Arita**

illustrated by **Jamie Tablason**

BeachHouse

On the island of Kaua'i in a small, dark cave
lived a sad dinosaur just staring at the waves.

Because of his size and the noises that he made,
all the creatures stayed away because they were afraid.

He would swim in the ocean where the sun seemed to end and dream about a day when he'd make a new friend.

He couldn't understand,
and often wondered why,
no one ever stopped to talk,
they would just pass him by.

But, watching from a distance,
every day after day,
was a small group of friends
about to ask him to play.

They huddled close together and approached him with care as the dinosaur watched them climb up to his lair.

At the mouth of the cave,
the group shouted out, "**HI!**"

"**COULD IT BE?**" thought the dino,
and he started to cry.

He ran and he yelled, **"I'M SO EXCITE**

"SO SORRY," he said,

"I HOPE YOU'RE OKAY?"

The friends laughed it off
and asked him to play.

TO MEET..." but the rumble from his running knocked them right off their feet.

They chased and they tagged, swimming circles 'round each other, telling jokes, sharing stories, having lots of fun together.

Little did they know that throughout these happy days the dinosaur was teaching them true Aloha ways.

When the mynah squawked unpleasantly
and was overall too loud,
the dinosaur said,

**"LET'S WHISPER
WHEN LOUD VOICES
AREN'T ALLOWED."**

When sliding down his long, scaly back
they quickly came to learn
the art of waiting patiently
until it was their turn.

On walks along the beach and up
a winding hiking trail,
the dinosaur stepped with care,
sweeping trash up with his tail.

And if they saw a sleeping seal or a cozy nest of eggs,
he made a protective space for them by stretching out his legs.

They learned that working as a team was always lots of fun.
Sharing ideas and trying things helped them get more done.

If he noticed someone struggling
with a very difficult task,
he'd say, "LET'S GO AND HELP THEM OU

BEFORE THEY HAVE TO ASK."

On special days, he went outside
and stretched his neck up high
and gathered all the coconuts to make haupia pie.

His first thought was of others because he really, truly cared.
He would always gather extra food so he'd have enough to share.

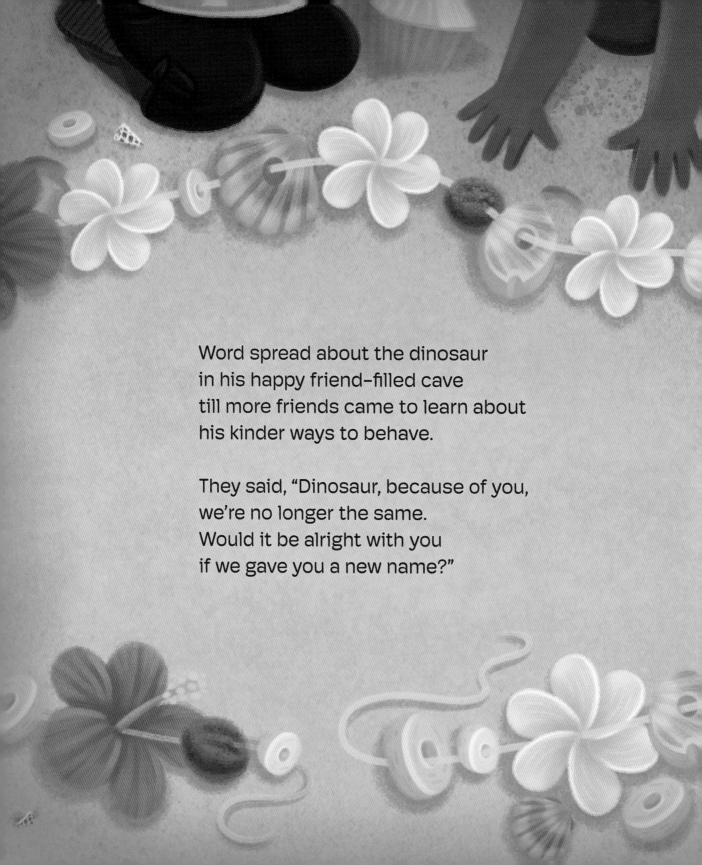

Word spread about the dinosaur
in his happy friend–filled cave
till more friends came to learn about
his kinder ways to behave.

They said, "Dinosaur, because of you,
we're no longer the same.
Would it be alright with you
if we gave you a new name?"

The group of friends gave a cheer
and hugged the brontosaurus.
"We've got the perfect name for you,
we'll call you **ALOHASAURUS!**"

So, Alohasaurus and his friends
spent their many days
living and sharing their aloha
in many different ways.

I praise God for His many blessings and for the hundreds
of former students who have modeled the ways of Alohasaurus!

E aloha kākou kekahi i kekahi.
(Let us love one another.)
—Vera Arita

For the Philippines.
—Jamie Tablason

ABOUT THE AUTHOR

Vera Arita grew up in Waipahu and received her bachelor's and master's degrees in education from the University of Hawai'i. She is a retired special education teacher and taught for over thirty-five years in Hawai'i. She and her husband have raised two sons and now dote on their three grandchildren. Her other children's books are *All Around the Islands, Can You Catch a Coqui Frog?, Animals Sing Aloha,* and *Alphabet Hukilau.*

ABOUT THE ILLUSTRATOR

Jamie Meckel Tablason loves illustrating for children and the young at heart. Through whimsical imagery and engaging characters, she hopes to connect with her audience and inspire everyone to tell their own stories. Some of Jamie's favorite things to paint and draw are yummy foods, weird animals, tropical vibes, old houses, and cool cars. She received her BFA and MFA in illustration from CSU Long Beach, School of Art. She currently works and lives in Lakewood, CA, with her husband and their two dogs.

Copyright © 2022 by BeachHouse Publishing
Illustrations copyright © 2022 by Jamie Meckel Tablason

No part of this book may be reproduced in any form or by any electronic or mechanical means, including information storage and retrieval devices or systems, without prior written permission from the publisher, except that brief passages may be quoted for reviews. All rights reserved.

ISBN 978-1-949000-25-2
Library of Congress Control Number: 2022940284
First Printing, September 2022

BeachHouse Publishing, LLC
PO Box 5464 • Kāne'ohe, Hawai'i 96744
info@beachhousepublishing.com
www.beachhousepublishing.com
Printed in South Korea